AF347024

*Count down the days until Christmas with this tale about
Santa Claus and Danish Christmas traditions.*

Pernille Meldgaard Pedersen

Him with the beard

Design: Pernille Meldgaard Pedersen
Editor: Emily Nemchick

© 2018 Pernille Meldgaard Pedersen
PMPstories
www.PernilleMeldgaardPedersenUK.blogspot.com

ISBN: 978-87-970862-5-4

I threw a little glitter here and a few spruce branches there, and with a high-pitched voice and the biggest smile on my face, I sang so loud the whole house shook.

"You better watch out! You better not cry! Better not pout, I'm telling you why! Santa Claus is coooooming to tooooown!"

Sausage, our chubby little dachshund, barked along with me. In my home, we loved Christmas. And not just loved – no, we LOVED Christmas!

Christmas was the best time of year, where the lights dispelled the darkness, where people were a bit kinder and where the lovely smell of clementines and spiced brown cookies drifted through the house. You'd never hear anyone say no to all the Christmas goodies. In fact, it was customary to have these in kilo bags, all served at once, while we all talked about how soon it would be January.

Like a kangaroo, I jumped onto the couch, trying to tie one end of the Christmas garland to the ceiling, but it wasn't a very effective method, because you can't jump and stand still in the air at the same time. On the other hand, it was really fun and mum-naughty.

I stopped my jumping when I, just my luck, heard the front door open. In came my two open-mouthed helpers.

Maybe I went a little nuts with the glitter?

HA! You could never have too much glitter!

"You're home!" I shrieked and threw my arms excitedly around my beloved family. Maybe I was also a little high already from the combination of marzipan, mulled wine and CHRISTMAS.

My nine-year-old daughter Mille saw me coming and backed away comically until she reached the wall.

I squeezed her in a hug.

"Not the sweater," she protested with flailing arms, her cheek completely mashed against mine.

Confused by her protest, I looked down at my best and most Christmassy sweater, with Santa in his sleigh pulled by his reindeer, and Rudolf's nose still lit up. Nothing strange to see here!

Kalle, my husband, kissed my forehead with a happy smile. "You've already started."

"Yep! And I need a strong and tall man to hang things up, and a strong and culinary Christmas girl to help me bake in the kitchen."

Three nudges of my elbow and a wink of my eye made Kalle move. Mille crossed her arms.

"I don't want to help." My heart almost stopped.

"What do you mean?! It's Christmas! Of course you want to help! I've bought the ingredients for all your favourite cookies! Vanilla wreaths, peppernuts, klejner! I've also found your sack so Santa knows where to put your presents."

"Santa? Just how stupid do you think I am? Santa is just

something you've made up. I know that it's Dad that puts the presents in the sack, and that it's Preben from next door who dresses up as Santa every Christmas Eve." Now my heart really did stop.

"But Santa does exist. He puts presents in the sacks when we're all asleep. You know that."

She rolled her eyes dramatically.

"It's true!" I protested.

"As if! Do you really want me to believe that there is a guy who's lived for thousands of years and just so happens to know all the children's wishes?"

"Why is that strange?" I asked confusedly. "We tell him our wishes in a letter, and..."

"And send it to the North Pole." She finished my sentence with barely concealed mockery, her arms crossed. "But why hasn't anyone found his house then?"

"It's supposed to be a secret. And also, the North Pole is a big island..." Her foot began to tap.

"And what about the toys? Why would he make copies of items you can buy?" Why so suspicious?

"Because that's what you've wished for?"

"And I suppose that the elves help him?" I shrugged. I assumed so.

"Reindeer can't fly," she continued. Now she was crossing a line.

"Santa's can."

"And where does he find them?"

"I don't know..."

"No, because they don't exist. And you can't know the answers to things that don't exist."

"You can just ask Santa when he comes. He knows where he found them."

"Mum, stop! Do you really want me to believe that?"

"But it's the truth!"

"Fine, then we'll say he 'exists'." My eyes widened in surprise when she lifted her hands and did quotation marks around 'exist'. I knew there was a first time for everything, but who taught her that?! "But then explain this," she continued. "How does one man manage to visit all the world's children on a single night?" I had to think about it for a bit.

"Well...you see, not everyone celebrates Christmas...and some countries have Christmas Eve on other dates..."

"That's still millions of children on a single night!" she shouted, making me jump. I had never seen her this angry before. "Mum, stop lying. Santa doesn't exist." She turned and stomped up the stairs to her room.

"Mille! Are you okay?" I called after her. A bang sounded when she slammed her bedroom door. Worried, I took the first step up the stairs to go see her, but Kalle stopped me with a hand on my arm.

"Better let her be."

"But something must have happened at school – she was looking forward to decorating this morning."

"She's probably just tired," he told me calmly, and tried to distract me by being distractingly charming when he found his old elf hat in the Christmas box and put it on.

On the couch lay our Christmas sacks. Kalle took his.

"Well, then I'll just hang my sack up in the usual spot, right next to the loft hatch. Then good old Santa won't have to carry my heavy gifts too far." He winked. He smiled when he finally got a smile out of me. Whistling, he went to the kitchen to hang his Christmas sack in the carefully calculated, strategic spot. When I was alone, I looked up the stairs with a strange feeling in my stomach.

Perhaps Kalle was right.
She was probably just tired.

It was the last weekend before Christmas Eve, and although most people associated it with Christmas stress and countless things to do, I instead used the time to enjoy the smiles and the joy my job brought forth.

Four weeks a year, I moved from being an office mouse at Vestercity shopping mall's office to helping in the mall Santa's cabin. World's best job multiplied a hundred times!

"Merry Christmas!" I sang and waved enthusiastically to five-year-old Emma, who was being dragged by her impatient big sister, who didn't want to wait any longer while she listed more thoughtful details about the elf dress she wanted for Christmas. I was smiling, entertained by the fraction I had heard. Red with white lace, and a secret pocket in the dress for elf sweeties. I was sure she'd get her wish fulfilled. She was a really sweet girl.

"Oh look! It's Santa!" announced a familiar voice passing among the many busy shoppers. It was the mother of one of Mille's friends. She stopped at the white fence that enclosed Santa's area. Right behind her was her own daughter, Olivia, and my Mille, who had joined them to do some Christmas shopping. I smiled and waved to them.

"That's not Santa," replied Mille in the same surly manner that she had adopted for the past three weeks about anything to do with Christmas. "It's just a man – and then my mother."

The energy that had kept me going flew out of me so fast that even my elf hat, which I had worn to be festive, lost its shape.

It was as if this December had gone completely wrong.

Normally, Mille begged to come and join me while I worked. In the morning, she would stand proudly, with big, excited eyes, in front of Santa's door in the dressing room, waiting for him to come out. And then when she alone had the honour of holding his hand and following him all through the mall and down to his seat in Santa's cabin, her eyes shone in a way that even I can't make them.

She had said that my job as Santa's helper was the best! But then last week, we had a quarrel where she accused me of deceiving the world's children.

I mean, sure, maybe there was some truth in it. After all, Claes was not *the* Santa. The real Santa naturally did not have time to stand in the shopping malls in December. But that didn't mean that he didn't exist.

"Do you want to go say hello to Santa?" Olivia's mother asked, looking at the girls.

"Please, Mum! We're not babies," Olivia replied, and rolled her eyes in a terribly familiar manner before grabbing Mille's hand and pulling her towards a jewellery stand. It looked like I had found the source behind Mille's change of heart.

Hmm. Would I be a very bad mother if I forbade her from playing with Olivia? She was clearly a negative influence!

Olivia's mother lifted her shoulders in a careless little shrug, not particularly shattered by her daughter's comment. I was shocked! No wonder her daughter behaved like that, considering her mother acted in the same careless way.

Before I forbade Mille to play with Olivia, I would forbid myself to spend time with Olivia's mother.

This conspiracy had to end.

"They grow up so fast," she continued with a sad little sigh. Confused, I nodded. I could only agree with her – although I didn't fully understand why it was relevant to the situation.

My attention was caught when a little girl started screaming and crying while she fought with her arms and legs against being placed on Santa's lap. Olivia's mother lifted her hand in farewell and quickly moved on. Claes, our Santa Claus, had many years of experience and laughed warmly till both daughter and father had settled down again. But the little extra time it took made the other children in the queue become restless. It didn't take long before I heard the first child who dutifully held his mother's hand asking if they could go home soon.

Across our little fenced area, I shared a look with my colleague, Puk. She quickly understood that we had to do something. We met in the middle, prepared to handle any situation that might arise.

"Ready?" she asked. We gripped each other's hands.

"Ready!" I beamed, and together we began to sing Christmas songs about Santa, and about the many things he had to do before Christmas Eve, while we danced and jumped on the spot. Our audience was no longer waiting impatiently. Instead they laughed, clapped and sang along in high spirits.

"We can hardly stand the wait. Please, Christmas, don't be late!" We finished the song, both breathless.

"Thank you, thank you, thank you," I sang while we both bowed in all directions to resounding applause. No matter where I looked, there was a big smile on everyone's face.

From the corner of my eye, I saw Claes call Puk to him. I thought nothing of it until Puk made an announcement, shouting out into the mall, "Santa is taking a little break! But I promise he'll be back soon!" Heavy sighs sounded from impatient children, who again asked their parents if *now* they could go.

Some people went while others stubbornly replied that they were waiting until Santa came back.

I shrugged to those who asked how long the break would be. I didn't know. We didn't usually take a break in the middle of it all. Confused, I went over to Puk, who looked relieved when I arrived.

"What's up?" I asked.

"Santa is sick. You have to help me. He can't stand up by himself."

"Nonsense. Of course I can," Claes protested. He struggled a bit, flailing his arms and legs, making it look much more difficult than it should be, but he managed to get to his feet. I noticed that his feet were dragging on the floor.

On the other side of the fence, a young disabled man stopped us. He was sitting in a wheelchair and had no way to enter Santa's small closed area because of the steps. He asked with big round eyes if Santa could please stay, because he wanted to talk to him. Claes smiled and patted him kindly on his shoulder.

"I'll be back, my friend. I just have to go look after my reindeer. If you don't keep an eye on them, they make such a mess." The young man laughed and told the story about the naughty reindeer to his mother, who stood next to him. I heard the beginning of an amazing tale just as Claes stumbled. Puk and I each grabbed an arm. This time he didn't protest when we offered our support.

It's was a sad sight to see. Santa was sitting hunched over, with a pale, sweaty face and his white beard and red coat discarded. Puk used a magazine to fan Claes, who clung to the bucket in his lap. I offered him a damp cloth and cold water, which he weakly accepted.

I couldn't help but admire how he had managed to stay in character all the way back through the mall to the staff area. Laughing, friendly and waving, he apologised to those who worried and begged him not to go yet without letting them see how sick he felt.

"Walking out in the middle of it all!" our boss Jens grumbled. He moved around in the little room like a tornado, charging left and right. I think we all tried not to take it personally. He was usually more hot air than anything else.

"I've never experienced anything like it!" he bellowed. "A real man does not get sick!" Claes got the last word by puking in the bucket. Jens grimaced and tried the phone again. I dabbed Claes's forehead with the cloth. He thanked me tiredly.

"Ole!" yelled Jens into the phone when someone finally picked up on the other end. "Put up a cancelled sign at Santa's cabin. Claes is puking everywhere."

Puk's face expressed the same emotion I felt: panic. There was no doubt that Claes wasn't in a fit state to do any more today, but we couldn't disappoint those who were waiting. There had to be an alternative.

I got an idea.

"We have a Mrs. Claus costume somewhere. Maybe Puk or I could..."

"No one wants to meet Santa's wife," Jens interrupted quickly. "I'd much rather have a puking Santa. At least it would get on Facebook if he puked on one of the children." He suddenly stopped and contemplatively looked Puk and me up and down in a way I really didn't like.

"But it would be something else if we had a sexy elf," he said. Gasp.

"Ha!" Puk snorted. "That's only going to happen in your dreams!"

Jens blushed. Claes and I echoed her protests.

"What about Dennis?" I suggested. "He could be Santa."

Jens shook his head.

"He's from Greenland!" I didn't understand what the problem was. He should be the perfect candidate, coming from the arctic circle. Who knows, maybe he and Santa shared ancestors.

"What about Ole?" suggested Puk.

"Too old!" replied Jens.

"What about William?" I suggested instead. William was perfect. He was always really helpful and really sweet too!

"William?! No, he's just a wee boy." Okay, then I'd just keep on thinking.

"What about Abdul?" I suggested. He was nice and neither old nor young. Ding, ding, we had a winner!

Jens looked unimpressed. "He's a Muslim."

"They don't like Santa?" I asked, baffled. Jens rolled his eyes.

"What if Stella wore the Santa suit?" Claes suggested. I heard the words that came out of his mouth, but they made no sense to me. And then they did. I stopped breathing. Jens's eyes were almost popping out of his head.

"No! That's the most ridiculous thing I've ever heard." I was relieved, to be honest. But Puk, the active feminist, continued in an offended tone.

"Why not? Is it because she's a woman?! A woman can be Santa."

"Santa Claus. Saint Nick. Father Christmas. Take your pick. They are all men."

"'Man' and 'human' are both the same in Latin. Women are humans!"

"No!" protested Jens strongly, his arms flailing in the air. "Hell no! Keep your nasty feminist hands away from Santa Claus. It's more than enough that you got out of the kitchen. What about celebrating that victory for a bit."

Puk roared and began a discussion with Jens – although it would probably be more precise to call it a war – about what Santa is, can and must be.

I was feeling more and more desperate because we weren't getting any closer to a solution that meant we didn't have to cancel.

Claes took my hand in his. He looked so weak and tired that I couldn't help but feel sorry for him.

"I can't imagine any better Santa than you, Stella." My heart jumped in my throat.

"Me?!" I screeched.

"Yes, my dear. Please put the suit on. We all need you." Talk about the pressure he was putting on my shoulders, because no. No, I couldn't. He didn't know what he was asking me!

Claes saw the protest on my lips and continued, unshrinking. "Please don't let the children down now. They've been waiting for so long and have so many things to say. It's important that Santa is there and listening to them."

"But they can tell you the next time you're there," I reminded him.

"But what if they lose courage?" he asked sadly. The very thought that some children needed to share things that nobody but Santa could understand made me catch my breath.

Unsure, I bit my lip.

"But what if they discover that I'm not a man? Then I'll ruin Christmas for them forever."

He squeezed my hand.

"Just smile, listen and be open. The rest will come from the children themselves." I doubted that, but the thoughts were already spinning in my head – I had to. I couldn't. I knew I should do it, but I didn't dare to.

Santa was one of the most important people in the world.

But he couldn't be everywhere at the same time. Someone had to be where the people were when he couldn't make it.

But what about Mille? And her friend Olivia, and the many other children who for some reason believed in Santa less and less every day. They would be proved right if I tried to fool all the children by wearing the suit.

I couldn't be Santa. It would be so stupid if I was.

But Claes's words were like an echo in my head – they had so many things to share, but maybe no one to share them with.

I had a hard time believing myself when I nodded okay to Claes. My decision was made out of fear for the consequences for those children. A female Santa was better than no Santa. I'm sure *he* would understand. Claes smiled proudly.

The pressure was heavy on my shoulders as I grabbed the red jacket and the puffy stomach and began practicing my deep voice and happy ho-ho-ho's.

I was shitting my pants when I approached the area with Santa's cabin. The queue had dwindled since we left, but there were still lots of children who met me with excited whispers and pointing fingers. I broke out in a cold sweat when I ho-ho-ho'd in greeting. It sounded so fake and hollow. They were going to discover that I was a scammer!

Jens didn't like to be outvoted, but he had grudgingly given his support and followed us. If there were any problems, I had no doubt that he would call someone who could come and help.

When I had taken my seat in Santa's chair, I nodded to Puk, signalling for her to let the first child in. It was a mother who placed her one-year-old daughter on my lap. She wanted a picture of her daughter with Santa. That was easy.

Next came two very talkative four-year-old twin brothers, both speaking over each other. They told me that they wished for racing cars that were faster than Santa's sleigh and showed me just how fast with their hands and made racing sounds to make sure I understood. They made me chuckle. Such funny boys. I reminded them that if they behaved well, Santa would come and visit them. As they walked away, they began quarrelling about whose car would be the fastest. When their disagreement ended with them wrestling, their mother had to intervene. With a firm grip on each of their shoulders, she reminded them that if they didn't behave well, Santa wouldn't bring gifts to them. Both boys looked back at me in horror. I wagged a forefinger at them in friendly reminder. They both nodded and took their mother's hands like the good boys they were. She threw a grateful smile over her shoulder as they walked away.

Puk opened the gate for the next child who waited. It was a boy of ten years or so, looking very much alone without his parents. When our eyes met, he lowered his to the floor.

I beckoned him to me.

"Come here, my friend." He moved hesitantly and stopped when there was still an arm's length between us. I moved to the edge of my chair to better hear him.

"What's your name, my friend?" He fiddled nervously at one of the buttons on his coat and mumbled his name. Gustav.

"Have you been a good boy this year, Gustav?" He shrugged. I was at a loss for what to say next. Was he quiet because of false modesty? Or perhaps he was a bully who wanted forgiveness from Santa, and if so, what was the procedure from here?

See, this was why I couldn't be Santa. I had no idea what I was doing!

I took a deep breath and decided not to panic yet. It seemed more likely that he was just shy. I knew how I could help with that.

"Do you want some candy? I have lots here in my sack..."

As I reached forward, he yanked my beard. I repeat: he yanked my beard!

My eyes were as big and shocked as his when the beard remained in place. I thanked my lucky stars (and Puk!) that the beard was tied so tightly.

Puk and Jens watched, gobsmacked, from the sidelines.

"Ouch!" I quickly improvised. Gustav, who had been rigid with surprise, jumped in fright and began crying.

"I'm so sorry, Santa!" he sobbed loudly, making everyone turn their heads to see what on earth Santa was doing to the poor boy. I began sweating again. "I didn't mean to be naughty, but I didn't know if you were real, and I need you to be real, because otherwise I don't know what to do."

My pulse was still racing at top speed, but the sight of the fat tears running down his cheeks and the agonized sobs that moved his shoulders up and down made me forgive him.

"It's okay, Gustav," I tried to comfort him. How could I blame him for trying? It could be difficult to believe – even if it was right in front of your own eyes. "What do you want for Christmas?" I asked him. With shiny eyes, he shook his head resignedly.

"I would like a dog." I was in a bit of a predicament. I didn't know if Santa gave pets. I had never heard of it before.

I wished I could ask Claes what to say. I didn't want to risk disappointing him if it was well known that Santa didn't give pets.

"A dog is a big wish and a big responsibility," I told him. He grimaced.

"Mum said that too, but I'll take good care of him," he promised me. "I'll walk him every day and give him food and play with him.

And he can sleep in my bed. I just want to have a friend. No one wants to play with me." I got a lump in my throat. Suddenly, I understood what Claes meant when he said that children had many things to share, and how important it was that someone was there to hear them.

I knew I didn't want to make promises I couldn't keep. After all, I was not Santa. But I could try – when I got home, I would write a letter to Santa, in the hope of making Gustav's wish come true.

"I'll do my best," I told him, watching as his whole face lit up with hope. Despite the fact that he had yanked my beard, I knew Gustav was the kind of boy that Santa wouldn't forget.

"Thank you, Santa!" he exclaimed happily, and gleefully hurried away.

"Gustav..." It suddenly flew out of my mouth. I didn't know what I was going to say. He looked worriedly back at me. The next words flowed off my tongue with ease. "I just wanted to tell you that you're not alone. I'll always be your friend." His shoulders looked lighter as he walked away.

"Stop!" I laughed with tears in my eyes, shaking my head at Kalle, who was cracking up, bent at the middle. "We really have to stop!" Kalle was wheezing for air as he tried to stop laughing, but every time we made eye contact, he started all over again. It was terribly contagious. And now my stomach and cheeks were hurting.

I had been excited all day to come home and tell Kalle all about my day. I knew he would love it, and he certainly did not disappoint. A few minutes into my story, he could no longer get a full word out through his laughter, and that set me off too. Every time I thought we were calming down, Kalle would shout, laughing, "and then he yanked the beard! HAHAHAHAHA!" setting us off again.

Kalle's shoulders still moved up and down in mirth, but his laughter was almost gone due to lack of air. He looked at me with bright eyes, shaking his head. I had to look away as he bit his lip to stop himself.

I felt giddy with happiness.

He dried his eyes, breathing deeply a couple of times, still half laughing.

"My wife, Santa Claus – who would have guessed it?" He kissed my lips and sang, teasing, "I saw daddy kissing Santa Claus..." I laughed.

"Eww, gross." The comment was from Mille, who stood in the kitchen door, wrinkling her nose. "You're embarrassing!" Kalle raised an eyebrow at me and smiled. Now it was my turn to bite my lip. Poor thing, to have such embarrassing parents. "Is the food done yet?" she continued.

Kalle and I shared a panicked look. We had forgotten all about his rice porridge! He hurried to the stove and stirred the pot, checking whether the white porridge had burned, making us all hold our breath until he announced in relief,

"Phew! No harm done. The porridge is ready. You can set the table."

Mille found the plates and spoons. Kalle placed the hot pot on the dining table and began to ladle the white porridge onto our plates. I found butter and sweet Christmas light ale in the refrigerator and smiled when I saw Mille sitting with the bowl of cinnamon sugar right under her nose and sniffing the sweet mixture. She licked her finger and dipped it in the bowl, making the tip of her finger turn brown and sweet. Kalle tutted and took the bowl from her. She giggled and licked her finger clean. Now I recognised my Christmas-loving Mille again. She took the box of matches that was lying on the table, lit one, and held it to the wick of the advent candle, which stood in the middle of the table.

A special calm settled over the room as the candle slowly but surely burned down a number, counting down another day till Christmas Eve. My pulse slowed when I looked at the flame gently playing back and forth. I sighed. Could this day be more perfect?

"You're smiling, Mum," commented Mille curiously, her mouth full. Her spoon hurried quickly back into the porridge again, digging lightly as she tried to get melted butter and cinnamon on the spoon too. I stroked her hair.

"It's been a really good day." And it became an even better day as she leaned her head against my hand.

"Why?" she asked.

"Mum replaced Santa Claus today!" Kalle exclaimed with great enthusiasm, giving me a wink.

Alarm! Alarm!

"Haha!" I hit him on the arm. Hard.

"Ouch! Why did you...?"

"Silly Dad! I did my Santa helping duties, just like I always do!" Kalle rubbed his arm with a hurt look. I signalled with my eyes for him to shut it. He crinkled his face in bewilderment. Gosh, how stupid could he be?

Mille was silent as she moved her spoon back and forth in her porridge. My heart was in my throat, beating a thousand miles an hour.

"What Dad meant was...that...Santa, you know, was...and he... kind of..."

"It's okay, Mum. I know he's not Santa."

"Of course he's Santa!" I exclaimed automatically. Mille glowered at me.

"I'm not stupid. I don't understand why you keep on lying. It doesn't make me believe it any more." I was ready to deny it, but her words stopped me. It was true that lies never benefited anyone.

"Okay," I relented, defeated. "Okay. The guy in the mall isn't Santa."

"That's what I've always said." She began eating again.

"But Santa is real! It's just because he's so busy, he can't be everywhere at once. We're just helping him."

Phew. That wasn't so difficult. Actually, it felt really good that she knew the truth. With the lie gone, she could finally begin to believe in Santa again!

She threw her spoon down hard on the table. The racket made me jump.

"Why do you keep making things up?! I'm not a child!" The chair scraped across the floor as she pushed away from the table and ran upstairs.

I was halfway out of my chair when Kalle touched my shoulder. He gave it a squeeze.

"Let me."

I watched the flame that had earlier brought me a sense of calm, but now was mocking and stressing me as the candle melted millimetre by millimetre as time went by, tightening the knots in my stomach. I blew out the flame and decided to wash up our plates. When they were clean, I took the pot and scrubbed and rubbed to get the burned porridge at the bottom loose, but even that didn't take long. I polished the stove so it shone like it hadn't done since it was brand new. I watered the plant in the kitchen window, and when I accidentally spilled some water, I dried it off.

But then there was a clean spot, so I ended up dusting all the visible surfaces.

When I opened the refrigerator and began to glare critically at all the shelves, I slammed the door again.

What was taking them so long?!

It was not that I doubted Kalle's abilities as a father, but sometimes there were things that only a mother could handle. That was at least the excuse that made me go upstairs. But I didn't get far. I stopped midway on the stairs when I heard my name.

"Mum is not trying to hurt you." From my hiding place on the dark stairs, I could see them both sitting on Mille's bed. Mille had her arms crossed, and Kalle hesitantly moved back and forth with Sea Lionel, her favourite teddy.

He nuzzled her foot with Sea Lionel, like we have often done over the years when she is sad. But instead of making her smile, she pushed him away. "Please don't be mad at her, Mille. Mum believes in him, and we have to let her do it."

"Then you're as crazy as she is! You don't really believe that he exists, do you?"

His silence stretched on for unknown reasons, and for that reason, I stopped breathing.

"Not like Mum does, no." I slipped back into the dark and down the stairs.

Five minutes later, Kalle came downstairs. He was smiling, but with tired eyes, and completely unaware that I was simmering like a pressure cooker.

He got a hint of the atmosphere when he didn't get a returning smile. He tried to ease the mood by wriggling out of the situation with charming comments, like, "How nice it is to have a clean kitchen," but the only thing that eased was the lid on the pressure cooker.

"Is it you who's filled her head with all that nonsense?!" I didn't like his tired sigh.

"What nonsense?"

"That Santa isn't real?!"

"Please, calm down, Stella."

"Don't tell me to calm down!"

"Listen, I know this is hurting you, but it won't lead to anywhere good. I have to put my foot down now. We have to think about Mille." I saw red. How dare he?!

"Are you really telling me that I'm a bad mother?!" He shook his head quickly.

"You're a good mother. That's not it at all."

"I think of nothing else but Mille!" My voice broke into a sob. The tears were right behind, and slowly but surely, my nose began running. He sat down on his knees in front of me.

"I know. Stella, I didn't mean it like that. But... Oh, Stella, I love you, I really do. The thing with Santa – I've always thought it was adorable, but now that it's creating a rift and hurting Mille... It has to stop. I know he means a lot to you, but it has gone too far. He doesn't exist, okay?"

"You don't know that for sure," I argued. I had a strong desire to remind him that he met Santa every Christmas Eve when he came to visit – but a little voice that sounded a lot like Mille's voice was ringing in my head. She'd said it was our neighbour Preben who was Santa. Why was that thought so impossible for me to believe when I knew and had accepted that Claes acted as Santa Claus at the mall?

"I know he exists," I repeated weakly. A stupid nagging feeling blocked my throat, so the words didn't come out as much more than a whisper. Kalle shook his head a little, but not in contempt. He felt sorry for me. My hands clenched into fists.

"He exists! And I can prove it!"

Mille snorted, standing in the kitchen door with her sports bag swung over one shoulder and her hockey stick by her side. I had forgotten she had a game today.

I hurriedly dried my eyes and smiled at her.

"Shall I drive you to hockey?" I had already got up and found the car keys when she answered.

"I'd rather have Dad do it." Kalle looked uneasily between us. Wounded, I handed him the keys. I evaded his kiss on the cheek, steeled myself against his hurt face, and looked bitterly after them as they walked out of the door and drove away in the car.

I'd prove that he was real.

And I knew just how.

I grabbed my coat and headed home to Mum.

"What a lovely surprise visit, my girl." Mum smiled as she came back from the kitchen with a full coffee pot. She turned off the lights on her way back and took a seat in her favourite chair. She poured coffee into our cups while I rifled through the many boxes of family pictures that have been taken over the years. Mum took a handful from the pile I had gone through.

"Oh look! Do you remember that Christmas? You had chickenpox and you..." I interrupted her quickly. She had a habit of talking for hours about the same thing if you didn't help her move on.

"Mum, it's not because I don't want to talk, but I'm looking for a very specific picture."

"Oh! Okay. If you tell me what's in the picture, maybe I can help."

"Do you remember that picture of me and Santa?" Mum went quiet. She blinked her eyes three times fast.

"I had it by my bed as a kid. Do you remember?" Blink, blink.

"Sure. But why is it important? Wouldn't you rather have one with Uncle Harry?" She quickly took a new picture from the pile. "Look, do you remember? That's when we were..."

"No!" I interrupted her fast before she completely disappeared into the memories. "It has to be that picture, Mum. Mille is mad at me, and Kalle, he..." My voice broke. Mum quickly put her coffee cup back on the table and took my hand in hers to comfort me. "He said something hurtful to me," I told her. "I need that picture to make everything all right again." She pursed her lips.

"It's just a picture."

"It's not just a picture!" I told her firmly. "It's my only proof that Santa is a real person!" She blinked, blinked, blinked, blinked, blinked. Suddenly she jumped out of the chair.

"Oh gosh! I completely forgot the cookies. We have to have cookies for our coffee." I grabbed her arm quickly before she left.

"It *is* Santa, right? The guy in the picture?" Her eyes looked away. "Mum, please. Who is it in the picture? You've always said it was Santa, but Mille and Kalle say he doesn't exist. I don't understand it. And now it's as if I have all these questions I don't understand." Time almost stood still before she finally reacted. She put one hand gently on my cheek, stroking a tear away that I didn't know had fallen.

"It was for the best, my dear." Her eyes teared up.

"What was?" My heart was beating rapidly as she walked to the chest of drawers and found an old shoe box hidden underneath tablecloths, napkins and candles.

I could hear blood rushing in my ears when she handed it to me. Her eyes didn't move from the box when I raised the lid with a dry mouth. Dizzy, I began to take the contents out of the box. Childhood drawings in abundance. Coloured lines that had made sense to me as a child, but now I would never be able to guess what they were supposed to be. 'Mum, Dad and Stella' an adult had written above what I would guess to be our heads. 'Four years' was written in the corner of the paper. I don't remember much from when I was four – only that it was the year we lost my dad. But when I say I remember it, it's mostly because my mother is always unhappy when we approach the dates of his birthday and the day he died. I realised that perhaps there was a reason why this box had been hidden away. I didn't want to hurt my mother.

Sniffing, she waved with her hand for me to keep going.

The next thing I picked up was a brown teddy bear that had clear signs of being worn and loved. I recognised it quickly and smiled, surprised. It was Oko! Or to be more correct, his name was actually Choko, but I found that difficult to say as a kid.

Oko had been so much a part of my childhood that I didn't quite understand how he had ended up in this box.

Along the edge of the box was a small pile of pictures. For every picture I leafed through, my heart sank more and more. They were all of Dad. Some before he got sick, him and me on a fishing trip, and a holiday picture at a campsite where he and I were playing football in front of our tent. It was difficult to look at the few that were taken when he was in the hospital. He looked ill and underweight, with hollowed cheeks and dark, tired eyes. They didn't shine anymore.

Everywhere I looked, tubes were sticking out from his body, connected to several machines next to his bed. Why did I have to see this?

I wanted to pack up the box again. What did this have to do with Santa Claus?

"Do you remember that it was Dad who bought Oko for you?" Mum asked, and as I often did with Sea Lionel to Mille when she was sad, she nudged Oko against my arm. But I wasn't a child. It wasn't sweet, not when I was so confused. I pushed Oko away.

"Did he?" Mum fell silent when she realised using Oko wouldn't help make this easier for me. She pulled her arms around herself, hugging Oko in the same movement.

"One day, when we visited him, he had been to the hospital's shop, all alone. It was amazing that he had left his bed. He had been bedridden for a long time..." She let the words hang there. But we both knew how it ended.

"But he didn't get well," I finished for her. With her wet eyes and compressed lips, she shook her head. A bittersweet memory for both of us. Oko shouldn't be in this box.

"The picture isn't here." I collected everything to put back in the box, but she stopped me.

"I know it's there. You have to dig further." When I didn't begin right away, she helped me. She took out a pile of red pieces of cardboard. Christmas decorations cut by a little child who hadn't quite mastered how to cut. She held up a hand. Her palm was completely covered with glitter. We smiled at each other. I clearly had equally fabulous taste regarding glitter as a kid.

"I should hang this on the Christmas tree," said Mum. "Right next to the one Mille gave me." She got up and did just that.

When I looked into the box again, my eyes widened in surprise.

Underneath the Christmas decorations was the image I had been looking for. With my heart in my throat, I took in everything I saw in the picture. I was embracing the big, smiling Santa Claus, whose cheeks were so red, so red. I myself had an almost manic smile because I was obviously so happy. In the background was a big Christmas tree with the lights on. The picture was like I remembered.

And then not, because this Santa didn't have the white beard or wear Santa's clothes. He was an ordinary man in his mid-50s with a greying beard. And the red clothes I remembered were in fact a red flower-patterned Hawaiian shirt.

What was going on here?

"Who's he?" I looked up at Mum. Her mouth tried to shape the words, but no sound came out. In almost no time, my idea of Santa had been ripped away. Lies. She was a liar. It was all a lie.

To my frustration, she kept on digging into the box instead of answering. She found a child-sized orange t-shirt and shook out the folds. Excess glitter floated in the air. She showed it to me as if it would explain everything. Irritated, I read the text on the t-shirt. 'The Home for Distressed Children's Sports Day 1982'. It told me absolutely nothing. My mother's face fell when she realised this.

"Are you going to explain, or are we going to wait until Christmas Eve?" I snarled as I stuffed all the treacherous things back into the box, where they should have stayed.

"I...I don't know where to start," she said.

"What about THAT YOU'RE A LIAR! Why in the world would you tell me that the man in the picture was Santa?"

"I didn't. You came up with that yourself." I rolled my eyes, much like Mille had done throughout the month of December.

"But you didn't exactly say the opposite either. Was it fun? To sit there and enjoy deceiving your child?" Bloody hell, I was only saying.

"What could I do? Should I really have extinguished that hope that Santa existed? He was very important to you. He gave you so much."

"I only believed in him because you said he was real! And

honestly, because he was 'important' to me? That's the worst excuse I've ever heard. He can't have given me so much that you still refuse to take responsibility for *never* telling me the truth!"

"It's not that simple, Stella." Try, I thought as I scowled at her. "I don't know if you remember when Dad died."

I gave up. Now she was dragging my dead dad into this mess. He had nothing to do with it. He was dead!

"After Dad died, we were both in a bad place. I was..." She took a deep, heavy breath. "I was completely broken and couldn't function. After some difficult months, and I'm not proud of it, but I couldn't take care of you. I didn't see any other option than putting you in care." She pointed at the t-shirt. It was not a story I had expected to hear.

"At the orphanage?" I shrieked, upset. Her eyes turned into little cracks of sorrow. "For how long?"

"About eight months." Eight months?! Wasn't it strange that I couldn't remember anything? After all, for a good deal of my fifth year I was away from my mother. Shouldn't it be imprinted on my brain as a terrible memory that would haunt me for the rest of eternity?

"I visited you as often as I could. It was me who took that picture..." She pointed to the picture in my hands. "It was a Christmas party at the orphanage. It was your last day there."

"Then you know who he is?" She nodded quietly.

"He was a helper at the home. His name was Ivan." Ivan? Not Santa Claus, Saint Nick or Father Christmas. But Ivan. A fairly average middle-aged man who really liked wearing red Hawaiian shirts. I felt so tired.

"It wasn't until we got home and you began talking about Santa that I understood that it was Ivan you were telling me about. You were so happy," she stressed, with eager nods. It seemed very important to her that I understood. I didn't nod along. "You wanted the picture of you two standing by your bed because it was Santa, and Santa had been your friend and you didn't want to forget him. When you talked about the man in the picture, your eyes shone in a way they hadn't done for a very long time. And every day you talked about him, dreamed about him, and hoped he would come to visit, your smile grew, and a weight lifted off both of our shoulders. He gave you something I couldn't." I had a lump in my throat.

"But couldn't you have told me when I got older?"

"You'll always be my little girl. I could never take your smiles away from you." Both of our eyes teared up.

"I'm sorry you had to discover it like this, Stella. I would have made it easier for you, but I didn't know how." I nodded. Of course I understood, but there was still a wish. A ridiculous little hope remained.

"So Santa doesn't exist?"

She became silent, biting her lip with doubt in her eyes before she responded.

"No, my darling. He doesn't."

A clink sounded when Kalle chucked the car keys in the key bowl in the hall. Mille's voice sounded happy as she told him about her hockey game. I took a couple of deep breaths and put on a smile before they reached the living room.

Kalle smiled when he saw me and shook his head lovingly as he saw me lying cuddled up with a snoring Sausage on the couch.

She might be a lady, but she snored like a roaring bear.

"Did your game go well?" I asked Mille gently, watching her smile slide off her face. She sneered with tight lips.

"Yes. Why wouldn't it go well?" Her voice sounded as if I had betrayed her by asking her this. Kalle told her to calm down. She ignored him. "Do tell," she continued with attitude. "Did you find evidence that *Santa* exists?" I shook my head and fought suddenly and desperately against tears that wanted to fall. Kalle saw this and, worried, asked the wrong thing.

"Are you okay?" I lost it and began bawling. Sausage woke up, and Mille looked shocked by my outburst. Kalle put his arms around me and comforted me like only he could.

But he was wrong.

Nothing would ever be all right again.

I wasn't proud of myself when I called Puk the next morning, telling her I wasn't coming to work. When she asked if I thought I had been infected by Claes, I answered yes without hesitation. She was sad that I couldn't join her on the last workday of the year and asked persuasively if I could please woman up and come anyway. I almost resented her because she was trying to tempt me with things that had never existed and meant nothing anymore. I wished her a merry Christmas and tried not to be affected by her disappointed voice. We had shared many hours as Santa's helpers for the last 14 years and shared our own traditions. She believed just as much as I did. Or as much as I had.

Tonight, after the mall closed, she would, without a doubt, as usual, break the rules and regulations when she climbed up on the roof of the mall and wished Santa a safe trip and a merry Christmas.

It used to be my favourite moment. Hidden in the dark, high above the city, just her and me and the city's glittering Christmas lights. Puk and I used to point out the best places where he could land with his sleigh and talk with such a childish freedom that I felt embarrassed now. I wondered if Puk really believed he existed? Or if she too just pretended, for my sake?

With her, up there on the roof, it had been easy to believe in magic, and that a generous, long-bearded old man existed.

Instead, I spent most of my day alone on the couch with the computer on my lap, my expression focused as my fingers quickly flew over the keyboard. Mille had previously asked me a lot of good questions about who this Santa was, and I felt a need to find answers. The internet seemed like a good place to start.

For each answer I found, new questions popped up, which I then wrote in the search box like one possessed.

For example, it didn't make much sense that we hung our Christmas sacks by the loft hatch. We had no chimney, so how would he even get into the attic? It was much more logical for him to use the door, but no, no. That's not Santa's way.

I found websites that backed up the idea of Santa Claus and came up with theories of how he managed to do all his work. But most of the answers ended with 'Santa Claus magic', and it was such a weak answer when I held it up against the websites that attacked the whole idea of Santa. They were at least well researched and well documented.

Imagine that somebody at some point sat down, thinking up this master plan that has given birth to the Santa we know today. Someone even made up that he should have his own laugh. How strange is that?

And in fact, when I started thinking about it, I decided ho-ho-ho was rather stomach-turning and scary.

Especially if you changed the pitch slightly.

I could hardly believe my own eyes when I found out that

Santa's stylist, the one who had decided Santa should have a big white beard and red clothes, was a soft drink company.

A company that had nothing to do with Christmas.

I slammed the computer shut and stomped into the kitchen to do something far more productive. I emptied the washing machine.

Christmas and Santa were just marketing ploys.

It wasn't a truth I had expected to find when I got up this morning.

In the kitchen window, I saw our car pulling into the driveway, and soon afterwards, Kalle and Mille entered the kitchen door wearing big smiles and carrying heavy shopping bags.

"We got all the food for Christmas!" exclaimed Kalle before he had crossed the threshold. He began to unpack the bags, taking out almonds, sugar, butter, cream, potatoes and turkey, and putting them on the table as if they were hunting trophies, laid out to be admired. I wondered how much he'd spent on food for the special and overrated 'Christmas'.

"Why do we actually eat turkey on Christmas Eve?" I asked sullenly. "We have meatballs in the freezer that need to be eaten." My question made both of them stop what they were doing. They looked at each other, baffled.

"Eh, what do you mean?" Kalle asked, faltering. "We always get turkey on Christmas Eve." I pulled a pair of trousers out of the washing machine and shook them to get rid of the wrinkles.

"But who says we have to eat turkey? Santa Claus?" Ha! As if!

I hung the trousers on the clothes horse and fished out a sweater from the washing machine. It got the same treatment as the trousers.

"It's just food, Stella," replied Kalle, wrinkling his forehead. "Why is it suddenly a problem? You like turkey and caramelized potatoes."

"That's not the problem at all!"

"Then I don't understand. Are you trying to say you'd rather have roast pork?" he asked, reaching for the car key lying on the kitchen table to quickly leave for the supermarket, where he would undoubtedly fight like a wild man against others, who didn't want turkey on Christmas Eve either, to get the last pork loin. Just to make sure that our Christmas Eve wouldn't be ruined.

But it was beside the point, because he would still call it Christmas food. Turkey, duck, roast pork – it's the same thing.

"I just can't see why we have to spend a lot of money on something that doesn't matter at all." I saw them share a look before I turned to work on my laundry. I could feel their eyes on my back.

I didn't understand what they found so hard to grasp. Christmas was a joke! Why did we celebrate Christmas Eve if it was not about Santa visiting?

While I speculated about this, to my horror, I saw a blue sleeve with snowflakes on it sticking out from the wet laundry in the washing machine.

Oh no.

Oh no! No! No!

I pulled the sleeve till the rest of the garment was free. My fears were confirmed when I saw that it really was my Christmas sweater. I didn't understand how I could have overlooked it in the laundry. It shouldn't even have been in the laundry as it was not washable!

With desperation, I pressed the button to see if the light on Rudolf's red nose still worked, but it didn't. And what was worse, the wool had started to unravel in several places. The more I touched the sweater, the more it fell apart between my hands. Very much like this Christmas.

I was howling as I left the kitchen.

It was the 24th of December, and Kalle had been trying all day to get both me and Mille off the couch to help get things ready for Christmas. There were lots of things to do in the kitchen, as well as setting the table or whatever else he said we had to do because it was Christmas Eve. Mille had turned him down right away and sat on the couch with her tablet, which tinkled and dinged once in a while when she won in her game. I followed suit and sat with the big plate of Christmas goodies in front of the television, spending some time looking for something that had nothing to do with Christmas. I ended up picking a crime show on Netflix. There is nothing like a murder to kill the mood. I unwrapped caramels at such a speed that before I had finished eating one, the next joined it. I wasn't enjoying what I saw on the television, or the sweets I ate.

I was feeling on edge. Why, I didn't know.

Restlessness?

Over-Christmas-excited?

I didn't think it was the last option mentioned.

It was just a very strange day.

What did I usually do on Christmas Eve?

The logical answer was that I usually prepared everything before Santa arrived. But since Santa Claus wasn't coming, it was obvious that I was not going to do that.

From my seat on the couch, I could see Kalle running back and forth in the kitchen. He looked really cute in his apron and the accompanying elf hat. Like a master chef, he was everywhere at once, stirring the pots while cutting the red cabbage. As he worked, he cheerfully whistled 'Jingle Bells'.

For a brief moment, I thought about joining him, but then the thought disappeared into thin air and my eyes drifted back to the TV screen. I began wolfing down sweets again.

Ten minutes later, Kalle suddenly stopped his chopping. It got my attention because he went to the kitchen window with a hand on his chin, looking outside in wonder. He began talking to himself.

"Who is that sneaking around outside?" Because we had been having trouble with thieves in the city for the last month, my thoughts went there first.

Kalle craned his neck, peering out the window to look for something that apparently was going around our house and into our back garden. From my seat on the couch, I stretched my neck to see what it was that had Kalle's attention. They had to be pretty stupid thieves if they were trying to break in while we were at home.

Just as Kalle entered the living room, a red hat appeared around the corner of the house, popping up over the tall rhododendron.

My heart kickstarted, running at 180 miles an hour in my chest.

He was here! He was really here!

Overjoyed, I looked at Mille – just as she rolled her eyes. She moved them back to her waiting game, and I remembered myself. The beating in my chest became a dull and cumbersome lump.

With a barking Sausage on his heels, Kalle walked across the floor and opened the garden door with a big smile.

"Merry Christmas, Santa! Mille, put that tablet away."

"Ho-ho-ho, my dear Kalle." I perked up my ears. Did I know that voice? "Merry Christmas to you too, my friend. And Merry Christmas to all." Not quite sure yet, I wished him a Merry Christmas.

"Are there any nice children who would like a Christmas present?" Kalle raised his hand lightning fast. Santa ho-ho-ho'd, while Kalle, in two seconds flat, tore the paper off his present. He cheered when he saw what it contained.

"Cool! New oven gloves! Just what I wished for. Thank you, Santa!" Santa took out a new present from his sack. Sausage was ecstatic when it was for her. It was a bone she could gnaw on blissfully all day long.

Didn't his sack look quite new and unused?

But perhaps it was necessary to replace the sack often, considering how many presents he handled.

"And here's one for Mille. There you go, my friend." She didn't jump for joy like Kalle and Sausage. She thanked him but then sat down on the couch again to play on her tablet. The present stayed put on the coffee table.

Santa Claus smiled kindly at me when it was my turn. My hands shook nervously.

"A present for my favourite." He chuckled. His boots squeaked as he went to give me my present. It was decorated with drawings of Santa Claus on the wrapping paper and tied with a white ribbon. My mouth was dry.

"I know you've been a good girl this year, so you get an extra special gift from me. For you, my good girl." I accepted the present, completely lost for words. Closer, I could finally see his eyes. They were friendly and smiling, but the only thing I could focus on was his boots. Rubber boots, similar to those that Preben always wore when he went fishing.

I didn't understand how Mille had figured it out, but she had been right all this time.

I was having trouble finding the right words.

I cleared my throat, my grip loose on the present.

"It's really nice of you, Preben." Preben ho-ho-ho'd.

"My name is not Preben. I'm Santa!" I tried to return his smile at his playful joke, but I couldn't keep up the charade. Behind his beard, Preben wrinkled his forehead, worried.

"I'm really sorry. Excuse me." I left the room in tears.

I'd never imagined I would go to bed early on Christmas Eve, but here I was.

"Are you okay, Stella?" Kalle asked carefully as he sat down on the edge of the bed. He tucked my hair behind my ear, finding a tearful face beneath. He let out a sad sigh. "Oh, honey..." I sniffed and ran a hand under my runny nose.

"Is he gone?" He nodded.

"He told me to send you his regards. He was very worried about you."

"Why did you invite him?"

"I thought it would make you and Mille happy."

"He must have been laughing at me." Like everyone else. Kalle was there to comfort me.

"On the contrary. I think he loves to be Santa." I scoffed.

"Why?" He shrugged.

"Why not? He makes people happy. Isn't that a good reason?"

"I don't feel happy at all."

"No," he agreed, hesitating for a long moment. "Mille is waiting downstairs. Join me?"

"I just want to lie here for a little bit." There was a long pause before his reply came.

"Okay." He kissed me on my cheek and went downstairs again.

In the silence that followed, I remembered the day I had been Santa in the mall. I couldn't say, like Preben, that it was something I loved to do. I had been scared at the thought of being exposed. And now, when I thought of the children who had trusted me, I felt a deeper kind of terror, like a leech had burrowed into my stomach and sucked all the joy out of me, leaving only fear.

Had I not promised the two twin boys a race car?

And what about Emma, the girl who told me that she was hoping Santa would come with an elf dress for her.

When I thought of the boy who wished for a dog because he had no friends, I could hardly breathe.

They'd be so disappointed tonight when their dreams didn't come true.

And it was all my fault.

I lifted my head from my pillow when a knock sounded on the door frame. In the door stood Mum, and by her side was Mille, fidgeting nervously. Mum smiled gently.

"I hear Santa has been here." If she expected to get the same happy response that I used to give her, she'd be disappointed. She got an unimpressed grunt in response.

Mille suddenly exploded into eager nodding.

"Yes, and he was really nice!" she said in an overly keen voice that didn't sound like her at all. "He had a present for me." Mum encouraged her by putting an arm around her shoulders.

"Did he? What did he give you?"

"New shin guards for when I play hockey," she said with a big smile.

"Sounds like a great present," Mum said. I saw her eyes quickly darting towards me to make sure I was listening. "Santa must have known that you really like playing hockey." I snapped.

"Don't talk to her like that! She knows that it wasn't Santa who gave her that present."

"Stella!" Mum berated me. Mille looked at me with big, fast-blinking eyes and left. I'm sure she appreciated me setting the record straight. Mum looked after Mille in concern and adopted her child-scolding position – one hand on each hip and raised shoulders.

"There is no need to use that tone of voice, young lady."

"What tone of voice? I'm speaking in the tone of voice that I always speak in," I continued with a tone that was slightly, just slightly louder and more high-pitched than usual.

Okay. I gave in.

I was using a tone of voice.

But who could blame me?!

Honestly, the last thing I needed was Mum telling Mille the same bunch of lies she had told me.

We didn't need that sort of problem, thank you very much!

Kalle appeared in the door. One look at him and you could tell he felt the tense atmosphere in the room.

He coughed nervously. "How's it going in here?"

"I know you're disappointed, Stella," Mum continued. "But it's unfair to the rest of us that you're being unkind."

"Unfair?!" I shot back, and in a few seconds, I was no longer lying horizontal in bed. I stood dangerously, like a broad-shouldered gorilla, at the end of the bed.

"It's you that has lied to me all of my life, and I'm not even allowed to react to it?! I thought we were supposed to be kind to each other at Christmas!"

They both hung their heads in shame.

"It was meant in the best possible way," Kalle apologised.

"I didn't mean to hurt you," Mum added.

And with those few words, all the fight left me.

Exhausted, I felt every fibre of my body fall back to earth with a bump.

Mum was right.

I wasn't being particularly kind myself.

Of course, I knew they had done it with good intentions.

Misguided good intentions, which unfortunately had caused me to lose all my Christmas joy.

The question of what we could do so I could get it back was hanging unspoken in the room. I had no idea.

Maybe I was now just one of those people who didn't like Christmas.

And maybe that was okay.

I felt empty on the inside.

Mum put her arms around me, clutching me in a hug. It was almost a relief, because I felt a heavy weight on my shoulders that I couldn't bear alone. How could you miss something that never was?

"I'm so sorry, Stella girl." She rocked me. "If I had known it would end like this, I would have told you a long time ago."

Someone knocked on the door behind us. I gaped when I saw it was Mille, dressed in a big Santa suit that hung in folds like a heavy curtain over her shoulders. She adjusted the pillow that formed the big belly up under the belt again before it fell out.

"Ho-ho-ho, are there any nice children here?" she greeted us.

"What are you doing, Mille?" I asked, perplexed.

"I'm not Mille! I'm Santa," she replied in the same way Preben had done. But that didn't mean it was a better answer. I looked at Mum and Kalle to see if they understood what was going on. They were both smiling. It didn't make me any the wiser.

In her hands, Mille held the gift Santa-Preben had given me. She handed it to me.

"Ho-ho-ho. Merry Christmas! I know you've been extra good this year, so you get an extra big present."

I was feeling dazed as I looked at the present in my hands. Mille signalled with excited eyes for me to open it. I loosened the ribbon and opened the wrapping paper. It was a new Christmas sweater with Santa Claus on the front. She indicated for me to press Santa's hand. Lights began flashing on the sweater, making it look like bright stars.

"I don't understand what's going on. Why are you dressed like Santa, Mille?" Her face fell.

"It's my fault you're unhappy." I turned into a mama bear. Whatever feelings I had before, they disappeared when I heard my daughter was sad about something that shouldn't be her concern at all.

"It's not your fault," I reassured her. "Not at all." She didn't look convinced.

"But it is. If I hadn't stopped believing in Santa, you would never have found out and then..." Full of shame, I interrupted her quickly.

"I would have found out sooner or later, Mille. It's not your fault. Or Dad's or Grandma's."

"Are you mad at me?" she asked. Her eyes were glistening. I hugged her.

"Of course not. I'm not angry with you or anyone else."

"But then why are you unhappy?" I had to think for a little before I felt I could answer.

"Because I don't know why we have Santa, or why we even celebrate Christmas anymore."

I had thought Santa was this understanding guy who brought joy and help to those who asked. But in my online search for answers, there was a lot of evidence that Santa was just a way for companies to make money. And it wasn't because I felt there was something wrong with buying and giving presents – after all, it was one of the things I also loved about Christmas – but I just felt that Santa deserved more than being used as a cash cow.

"But if you knew the answer, would you be happy again?" Mille asked with a light in her eyes that I recognised. It was the light she had been missing all December. Warm in my heart, I stroked her cheek. My sweet little girl.

"Maybe, but it's not something you can find an answer for, and that's all right." And although I still had a little empty feeling inside, I wouldn't allow it to divide me and my family.

Suddenly Mum cleared her throat.

"For me, Santa gives me room to breathe," she said, nodding to herself and then to us. "He gave you and me the opportunity to get away from all the sadness and begin a new life together. Hope and space," she repeated.

She looked over at Kalle, who quickly caught the ball.

"To me he's joy. There's so much excitement and so many tales surrounding him. It's not Christmas until he has mysteriously put something in our Christmas sacks, left footprints outside our house and eaten the rice porridge we've left out for him. He spreads joy and expectations." I smiled gratefully at them.

Mille looked desperately back and forth between us.

"I don't know who Santa is." I gave her a hug and told her it was okay. She sniffed.

"But I'm sorry I've been so stupid throughout December, because it meant I didn't get to celebrate Christmas with you." I squeezed her in a hug. She surprised me by squeezing back. Oh my, here came the tears. Happy ones this time.

"So perhaps Santa is you and Mum together?" suggested Kalle.

Mille gave him a thoughtful look.

"Maybe." She nodded and looked at me. "I'm sorry, Mum. It has been a very strange December." I understood what she meant, as I had thought the same thing earlier.

It was also then that I suddenly saw myself in Mille. We had shared the same pain, but where I had support from Mum and Kalle, she had been smothered by a mother who didn't want to realise she was wrong. I was ashamed of myself.

Despite all this, Mille had dressed up like Santa, just to cheer me up.

I understood now why Mum and Kalle had smiled proudly at her.

I looked at my family and realised something that was magical and gave me the joy of Christmas back.

Maybe Santa wasn't real. And a lie too. But Santa was still something very special.

Every time I needed him the most, he was there. When I was a child, he came in the shape of Ivan. And now here he was today, in the shape of Mille.

Something Claes had said when I was Santa came back to me. He had said that I shouldn't worry, because the kids do the rest. The 'rest' seemed so vague, and it felt too easy to do something wrong, but suddenly I understood what he meant, because Mum and Kalle had just given me the answer. For some, Santa was one thing, and for others, he was something else. He helped those who believed because they let him do it.

To me, Santa was love. I understood that now, looking at my family who had lied to me because they wished me the best and never meant to hurt me.

Because they loved me.

Just as I loved them.

And as long as there was love, I knew Santa would always come to visit.

The End

Newsletter

Do you miss Stella already?
Everyone that sign up for my newsletter
will be sent the exclusive FREE short story
"When Kalle met Stella"

Sign up at my website or be updated about the exciting things
happening in Vestercity via social media:

website: www.PernilleMeldgaardPedersenUK.blogspot.com
facebook: Pernille Meldgaard Pedersen - Author
twitter: Pernille56
instagram:PernilleMeldgaardPedersen

Acknowledgements

There are so many people I need to thank for this story being published.

First and foremost, my mum, who is always there with comfort and encouragement when I need it. It's because of her that I found the courage to publish this story.

Thank you to Santa Claus for finding the time to visit my family every year. We look forward to you coming again this year!

Thank you so much to my editor, Emily Nemchick, who was a big help in getting this story ready in English. She ironed out the sharp edges of my sentences and got the magic I saw in the story to shine.

To all the bloggers who were enthusiastic when I contacted them and who reviewed my book. Thank you so much for all your support.

A shout out and huge thank you to these bloggers: Dawn from Crooks on Books, Sharon from Shaz´s Book Blog, Stacy from Stacy Is Reading, Laura from Laura Patricia Rose, Simona Elena from Simona´s Corner of Dreams. Thank you for letting my blog tour visit your beautiful blogs.

Thank you to Paige Toon for reading my story and for loving it.

And an extra thank you to Paige Toon for giving me Johnny Jefferson.

And finally, a huge thank you to everyone who read this story. If you loved this story, please leave a review wherever you purchased it. It's one of my wishes for Christmas ;-)

About the author

Pernille was born in 1988 and loves that she was born in the decade
with the tallest hair, the most colourful clothes, and the best music.

Her imagination never stands still, and
it's often expressed in words and pictures.

She wrote her first story when she was six years old.
It was about the cat she unfortunately never got
but wished for more than anything.

She loves autumn and Christmas and believes in elves.

From day to day she is a knight in training, an animator, and a
secret agent – she has saved the world a few times by now.
She's also a professional daydreamer.

She thinks the recipe for a good book is the same as the one for
having a good life – a sense of kinship, humour, love, and that one
thing that gives you a daily smile.

Vestercity is a fictional city based on her upbringing
near the city of Herning in Denmark.